A first boo

The day the clocks stopped

Written by William Geldard
Illustrated by Jolyne Knox

PUBLISHED BY THE READER'S DIGEST ASSOCIATION LIMITED

Timothy Tumblespring
is the busiest person
who ever lived.
His job is making sure
that everything happens
at the right time.
He makes the sun shine
in summer
and the snow come down
in winter.
He makes the leaves fall
in autumn,
and the flowers grow in spring.
And he looks after
all the clocks in the town.

NORTH WIND

Big ones that go
DING! DONG! BONG!
And wake up the town
at three o'clock in the morning.

Little ones that go

tick tick tick tick tick tick tick tick tick tick tick tick tick tick tick,

and let you sleep
till half past nine or later.

Just imagine what trouble
there would be
if ever Timothy
got things mixed up!

One day, the four winds
thought they'd play
a trick on Timothy.
"I'll make him soaking wet,"
said the West Wind.
He huffed and he puffed,
and blew up a great storm,
with thunder and lightning,
and sheets of rain.
But Timothy put up his umbrella.
And so he kept dry.

"I'll freeze him,"
cried the icy North Wind.
He huffed and he puffed.
All the ponds froze over.
And icicles hung by the walls.
But the more the wind blew,
the more Timothy hugged
his overcoat around him.
And so he stayed warm.

"I'll blow him over,"
said the fierce East Wind
He huffed and he puffed.
The trees bent right over,
and lost their leaves.
But Timothy ran into his house.
He bolted the door,
and so he was safe.

"I'll send him to sleep,"
said the warm South Wind.
He blew very gently,
more a whisper
than a huff or a puff.
Old Timothy felt his eyes go heavy.
And he nodded off to sleep
in the middle of the day!

He slept on and on
for a whole day!
A whole week!
A whole month!
A whole year!

All the clocks in the town came to a stop.

Except for one,
and that was Timothy's
magic clock.
But still Timothy dozed away.
What do you think happened?

The birds didn't wake
and start to sing
in the morning.
Instead, they waited until
the moon was high in the sky,
and the stars were out.

The sun stayed in bed
until ten in the morning.
So everybody slept late.

The days of the week
got all mixed up.
Children played in the street
on Monday,
instead of going to school.

And they all went
to school on Sunday,
only to find that
the classrooms were closed.

It snowed in the middle of August, when everyone was on holiday.

But in winter,
when all the children
longed for snow,
it stayed sunny for weeks.

Christmas Day was in the middle of the summer.

Worst of all,
nobody could have a birthday,
because all the birthdays
were mixed up, too.
Everything was topsy turvy
while Timothy slept.

But those four naughty winds
had forgotten one thing.
And that was
Timothy's magic clock.
"Things have gone far enough,"
thought the magic clock.
And nearly burst itself with
the loudest alarm you ever heard.
BRRRINNGGGGG!!

Timothy woke with a start.

He shouted at the four winds.
And they scampered away
with a whoosh.

Then Timothy put everything back as it should be.

The birds woke up
and started to sing
at five o'clock in the morning.

All the children in the town
were out of bed by eight o'clock.

The days of the week
got smartly back in order.

January
February
March
April
CHART
May
June
July
August
September
October
November

The trees put out
fresh green leaves in spring.

And the sun blazed down
from a clear sky in summer.

The leaves turned red and gold
in autumn.

And the world turned white
in winter.

But best of all,
Timothy made everybody's
birthday happen on
the right day.
So everything was just as
it always had been before.
I think that's best.
Don't you?

MY FIRST LIBRARY

Printed in Hong Kong